Don't count the number of birthdays. Count how happy you feel. I'm Birthday Bear, and I'll help make your birthdays the best ever.

I'm Wish Bear, and if you wish on my star, maybe your special dream will come true.

If you're ever feeling lonely, just call on me, Friend Bear. See, I've got a daisy for you and a daisy for me.

Grr! I'm Grumpy Bear. There's a cloud on my tummy to show that I take the grouchies away, so you can be happy again.

I'm Love-a-Lot Bear. I have two hearts on my tummy. One is for you; the other is for someone you love.

It's my job to bring you sweet dreams. I'm Bedtime Bear, and right now I'm a bit sleepy. Are you sleepy, too?

Now that you know all of us, we hope that you'll have a special place for us in your heart, just like we do for you.

With love from all of us,

The Care Bears

Care Bears, Care Bears Logo, Tenderheart Bear, Friend Bear, Grumpy Bear, Birthday Bear, Cheer Bear, Bedtime Bear, Funshine Bear, Love-a-Lot Bear, Wish Bear and Good Luck Bear are trademarks of American Greetings Corporation, Parker Brothers, authorized user.

Library of Congress Cataloging in Publication Data: Cowell, Phyllis Fair. Your best wishes can come true. A Tale from the Care Bears. SUMMARY: Because his name and size are similar, second-grader Jimmy Little has to contend with the teasing of his classmates until Wish Bear helps him realize his dearest wish.
[1. Wishes—Fiction.   2. School—Fiction.   3. Bears—Fiction]   I. Title.   II. Series.
PZ7.C8354Yo   1984   [E]   83-23726   ISBN 0-910313-18-0
Manufactured in the United States of America   5 6 7 8 9 0

A Tale from the Care Bears

Care Bears

Your Best Wishes Can Come True

Story by Phyllis Fair Cowell
Pictures by Joe Ewers

Jimmy Little ran all the way. He wanted to get to school early. The last day of school was sure to be different. Today all the books would be put away and maybe, just maybe, some of the kids would put away the ideas they had about him.

Jimmy's teacher, Miss Kirk, was already there.
She carried an armload of boxes.

"I will help," Jimmy offered. He liked to
help out.

But then the door opened and more children ran in.

"We can do that," they shouted, and snatched all the boxes from Jimmy. "Little Jimmy won't be much help."

"Jimmy Little," Miss Kirk corrected them.

"Sure," they agreed. "Little Jimmy Little."

Jimmy shoved his hands into his pockets and stared at the floor. He wanted to hide deep inside himself. But all he could hide were his hurt feelings.

All year Jimmy had been called "Little Jimmy." For Jimmy Little was just like his name. He was the smallest boy in second grade.

Jimmy had red hair, and Jimmy liked to read books. But nobody ever called him "Red" or "Books." They only called him "Little." And that's the way they treated him.

He was always one of the last chosen for baseball . . . almost the last picked for football . . . and the very, very last for basketball.

No one really tried to be mean. Except maybe
Darren, the tallest boy in second grade. Once, he
held up the class rabbit next to Jimmy and said
that the rabbit was bigger!

So the last day of school was no different from the first day of school, until Miss Kirk announced, "Soon it will be the Fourth of July. Part of the town celebration will be a race for all second graders. If you want to be in it, put your name on this paper."

Jimmy loved to run races. Sometimes he raced his father all the way around the pond. So Jimmy wrote his name right under Darren's.

After school Darren asked, "Why did you enter the race? You don't have a chance."

"Oh yeah?" Jimmy said bravely. "When I race my father around the pond, I always win!"

Darren just laughed. "You mean he lets you win. Grown-ups always do that."

Jimmy began to worry.

In the evening, Jimmy helped his father make supper. "Dad," Jimmy said slowly, "tell the real honest truth. When we race, do you just let me win?"

"The real honest truth," his father repeated. "Well . . . sometimes, I guess."

After that Jimmy could eat no supper at all.

That night Jimmy could not go to sleep, either.
He looked out at the brightest star in the sky and
made a wish.

"Oh star, I wish someone could help."

Suddenly, the star seemed to fall across the sky and right through Jimmy's window.

"Wow!" Jimmy said in surprise.

"Wow, indeed!" echoed a small voice behind him. "That was quite a trip."

Jimmy spun around and saw the star on the tummy of a cute little bear.

"I'm Wish Bear, and I was just wishing, too," said the bear. "I was wishing someone needed me. And look, you do."

"Then, a wish can come true?" Jimmy asked

"Of course," nodded Wish Bear. "Some wishes come true right away. But some do take longer. You just have to keep wishing."

"I've got lots of wishes," said Jimmy, "I wish people would stop calling me Little Jimmy Little."

"They will," assured Wish Bear. "Just give them time."

"And I wish they would stop treating me in such a little way."

"Don't treat yourself little, and they will soon see past your size," Wish Bear said.

Jimmy had another wish but did not know if
he dared make such a big one. So he said it quickly.
"And I wish I could win the Fourth of July race."

"Well, now!" said Wish Bear. "A wish like that
is no good unless you try. You have to help it along
with your very best effort."

Jimmy was beginning to feel much better. "I'll
tell you what: Why don't I stay around until after
the race?" said Wish Bear. "Now you go to sleep."

The next day was the first day of summer
vacation. In the morning, Jimmy felt so good he
flew his kite. But soon the kite met a tree, and
there it stuck.

Jimmy thought of what Wish Bear had said, about giving your very best effort. He stood on tip-toes, and stretched until his fingers touched the kite.

"I got it!" he thought happily.
Then someone tall pulled it down.
"Here you go, Little Jimmy," said his tall,
teenage neighbor. "You can't reach that high. I
don't know why you even tried."

Jimmy's face turned as red as his hair. Suddenly, he jumped up and down on his very own kite. When it was all bits and pieces, he ran into his house.

"What's the matter?" asked Wish Bear, who was sitting on Jimmy's chair.

"People don't think I can do anything," Jimmy cried. "I wish . . . I wish . . ."

"Go on," Wish Bear urged. "What do you wish?"

Jimmy gulped. Then he whispered. "Sometimes I wish bad things. I wish everyone else was just four inches tall. Then I could jump up and down on them."

After he said it, Jimmy felt so bad he hid his face in his hands.

"It's all right," Wish Bear said. "We all have mean wishes sometimes, especially when we feel angry or hurt. But we're happy when they don't come true. Just remember, the better the wish, the better the chance it will come true."

"I don't think any of my wishes have a chance," Jimmy sighed. "I will always be Little Jimmy Little. And I will never win the race."

Wish Bear tried to make Jimmy feel better.
Each day she ran around the pond with Jimmy.
But Jimmy never ran fast. He never really tried.

The Fourth of July dawned sunny and warm. But Jimmy would not get out of bed.

"Come on, Jimmy," Wish Bear called. "It's the Fourth of July. Today is the day your wish can come true."

"Or today is the day that it won't," Jimmy moaned. "I don't think I feel so good."

"I think I know how you feel," said Wish Bear. "Maybe a little bit scared and a little bit worried."

"A little," Jimmy agreed. "But it would take something big to make me feel better."

"Like a Birthday Party?" asked a voice as warm and sunny as the day.

Jimmy blinked. Now there were two Care Bears in his room.

Wish Bear giggled. "This is my friend, Birthday Bear. He loves to celebrate birthdays."

Birthday Bear was excited. "Today is a great day to celebrate. The Fourth of July is one huge birthday party."

"Whose birthday?" asked Jimmy.

"Why it's the birthday of this great country, of course. There are parties in each city and town, cake and ice cream, hot dogs and cold drinks. Ahhh!" sighed Birthday Bear.

"I always have fun at parties," said Jimmy.

"And when you have fun, you don't worry,' said Wish Bear.

"The race is just a party game," Birthday Bear chimed in. "Like pinning the tail on the donkey, or musical chairs."

"Well . . . " said Jimmy, now thinking of ice cream and hot dogs and games. "Maybe we should at least go."

Wish Bear and Birthday Bear settled down in the tall grass. "We will stay here out of sight," said Wish Bear.

Jimmy brought them cake and ice cream, and he went off to play horseshoes. Then someone announced, "And now, for the BIG race."

The word BIG made Jimmy shake as he stood with the other runners. He tried to look to the finish line. But all he could see was the back of a head, and the back of a head, and the back of another head.

"Ready, set . . ."

Jimmy felt smaller and smaller.

Then he remembered his wishes. When the runners took off, he ran faster than he ever did before. Soon others were looking at the back of Jimmy's head. Only one more was still in front— the tallest boy in second grade. Jimmy ran harder.

Darren was surprised to see Jimmy right beside him. He ran faster.

Jimmy ran faster.

But Darren ran faster still. He took one long
leap and crossed the finish line.
Darren had won the race.

Jimmy felt very disappointed and hurried away to the tall grass and his bear friends. But all he found there was some stardust, and a small piece of birthday cake. Jimmy felt all alone, little, and sad.

"Hey, Jimmy Little!" a voice called out.
It was Darren. Jimmy started to run away.
"Don't run," Darren yelled. You've got the
fastest feet in town . . . besides mine."

"Little Jimmy Little?" asked another second grader.

"Not *Little* Jimmy Little," said Darren. "*Lightning* Jimmy Little. Or maybe we should call him Flash Fast Feet."

Jimmy grinned. He liked those names much better.

Darren put his feet next to Jimmy's. "I guess you don't have to be big to be fast. You proved that today."

Jimmy thought about what Wish Bear had said. Some wishes come true right away. But some do take longer.

"And next year I'll win!" Jimmy laughed.

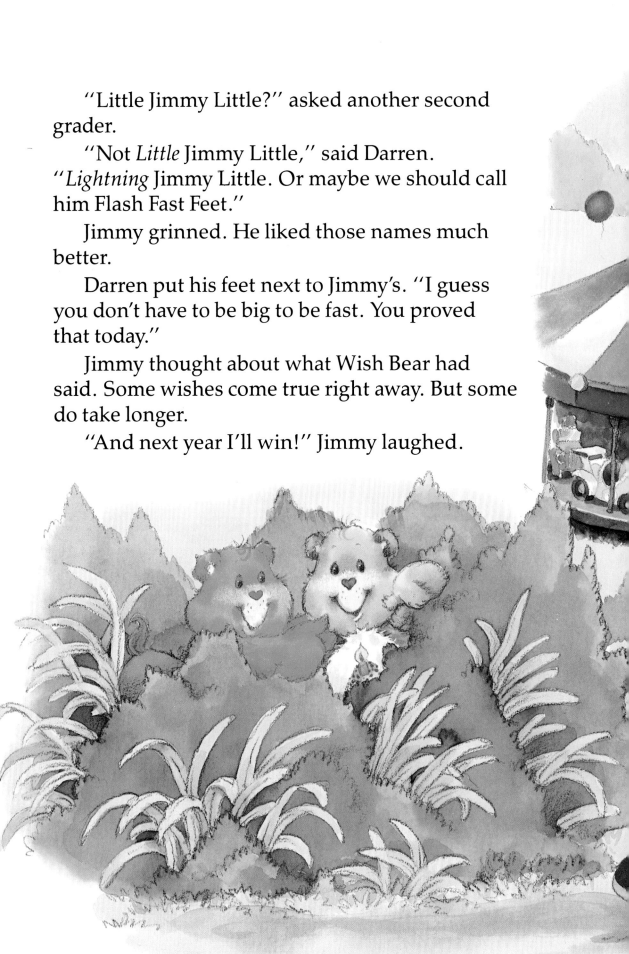

That night, Jimmy and his friends watched the
fireworks that celebrated the country's birthday.
Sparks of color burst in the air.

One looked just like a birthday candle, and
another—a wishing star.